I'M STICKING WITH
YOU TOO

For Tom – who is **perfectly** amazing,
and who makes my heart sing for joy – S.P-H. xx

To friends old and new – S.S.

SIMON & SCHUSTER
First published in Great Britain in 2021 by Simon & Schuster UK Ltd
1st Floor, 222 Gray's Inn Road, London WC1X 8HB

Text copyright © 2021 Smriti Prasadam-Halls
Illustrations copyright © 2021 Steve Small

The right of Smriti Prasadam-Halls and Steve Small
to be identified as the author and illustrator of this work has been
asserted by them in accordance with the Copyright,
Designs and Patents Act, 1988

A CIP catalogue record for this book is available from
the British Library upon request

ISBN: 978-1-4711-9319-4 (HB)
ISBN: 978-1-4711-9320-0 (PB)
ISBN: 978-1-4711-9318-7 (eBook)

Printed in China
1 3 5 7 9 10 8 6 4 2

I'M STICKING WITH YOU TOO

Smriti Halls and Steve Small

SIMON & SCHUSTER
London New York Sydney Toronto New Delhi

**Wherever you're going,
I'm going too,**

**WE fit together,
just me and you.**

We're perfectly tuned,
we just get along,

We make merry music,
we sing the same song.

Hey, what you doing?
I'd like to play!

Yes, well you can't,
so please go away!

But this looks like fun,
I'm really good.

Hmph! We REALLY
don't think that you should!

Come on!
Please, please?

This SO isn't fair.

Well, it's not up to *me* . . .
it's up to BEAR!

Go on, just once,

just one teeny go?

Well,
I would say yes . . .
but *Squirrel* says NO!

Hello!
How's it going?

Hello! Only me!

Hello!
There you are!

Hello! Cup of tea?

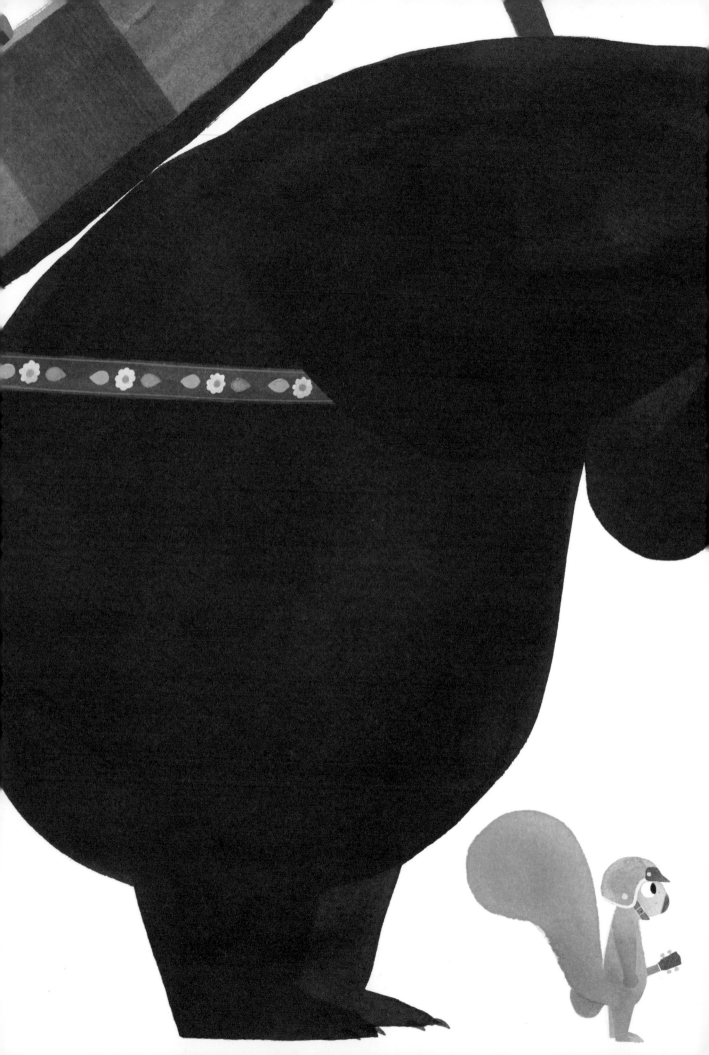

Look, Chicken, we're sorry,
you're perfectly sweet,
But you don't have the rhythm,
you don't have the beat.

Plus . . .

Your strut's out of step,
your cluck's MUCH too loud,

And two is just perfect, but . . .

. . . THREE is a crowd.

Well!

If that's how you feel,
I'll go my own way.

*I'll find a NEW crowd
who want me to stay . . .*

*Who'll welcome
me in . . .*

. . . and call me their mate.

Who'll REALLY and TRULY
think that I'm . . .

. . . great . . .

Don't worry, Squirrel,
everyone knows
we weren't being mean,
that's just how it goes.

I know you're right, Bear,
I quite understand.
We've only got room
for two in our band.

We can't be a three,
I mean,
come on,
hello!
Three doesn't fit,
it just doesn't go.

WE are a pair,
THAT'S how we stick.

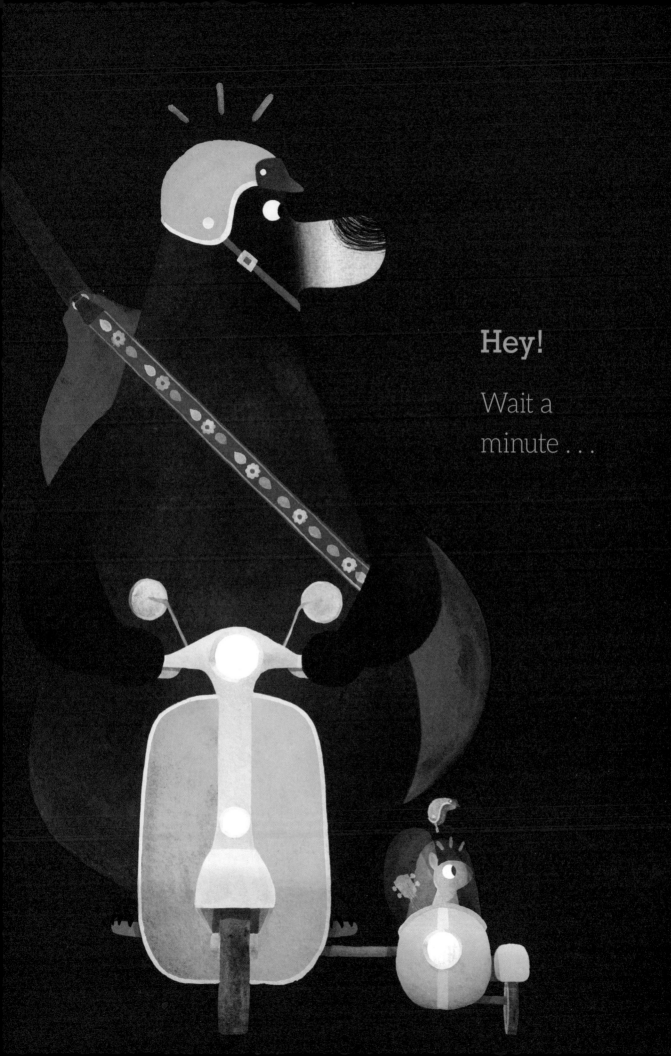

Hey!

Wait a
minute . . .

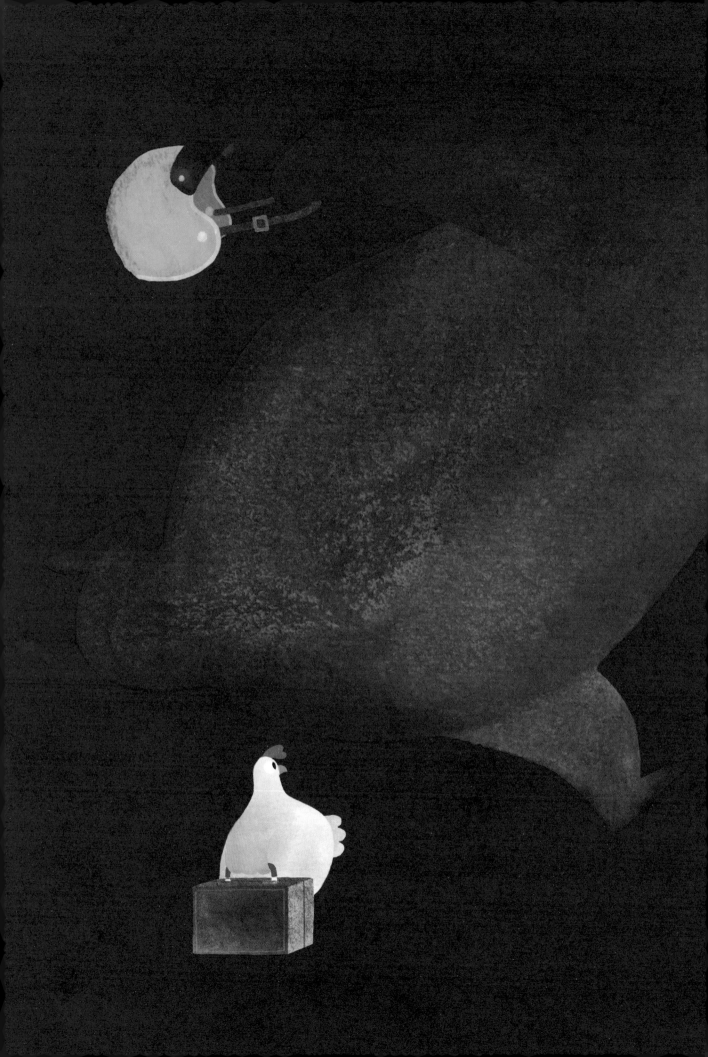

OI, THAT'S OUR CHICK!

What a pair of silly old twits,
Why couldn't we see
that more than two fits?

Some things work out
when we do them
TOGETHER.

Two can be good,
but three can be
BETTER.

Three is a team,
three is a pack.

Three means don't worry,
we've got your back.

**Three can be messy,
but why should we care?**

Three has got STYLE,
three has got FLAIR.

Sometimes we'll get our tune in a tangle,
our notes in a knot,

our jam in a jangle.

**But though quarrels
can shake us,**
and threaten to
break us . . .

They'll never,

they'll never,

they'll NEVER

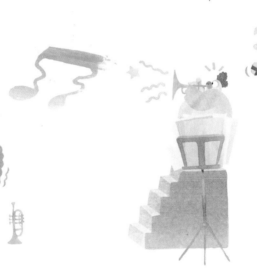

unmake us.

HA

HA

HE
HE
HE

HA

HA

HA

HA

Because WE fit together
like beats of a drum,

*Like the chorus
of notes in the chords
that you strum.*

Like the toot
of the tune
that makes
your toes tappy,

Like the la-la-la-la that makes your heart happy.

We make our own music,
we've nothing to prove,

**We do our own thing,
and find our own groove.**

Because we know . . .

*You can flap your
own feathers,*

And sing your
own song . . .

When you know
in your heart . . .

. . . that you *truly* belong.